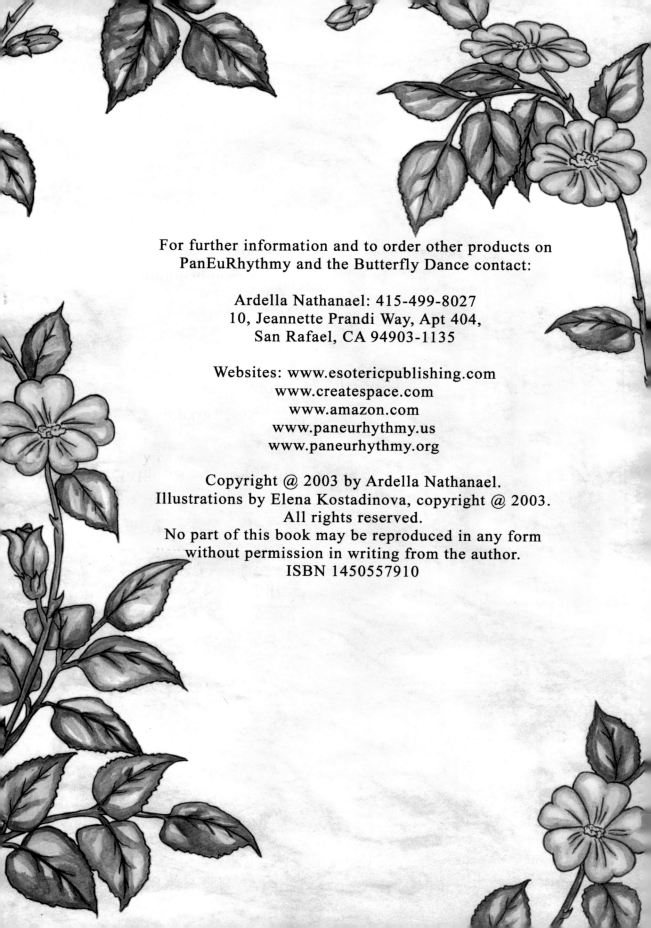

For further information and to order other products on
PanEuRhythmy and the Butterfly Dance contact:

Ardella Nathanael: 415-499-8027
10, Jeannette Prandi Way, Apt 404,
San Rafael, CA 94903-1135

Websites: www.esotericpublishing.com
www.createspace.com
www.amazon.com
www.paneurhythmy.us
www.paneurhythmy.org

The Butterfly Dance

Peter Deunov's PanEuRhythmy

Text by Ardella Nathanael
Illustrations by Elena Kostadinova

Music by Peter Deunov

English Lyrics by
Vessela Nestorova
and
Barnaby Brown

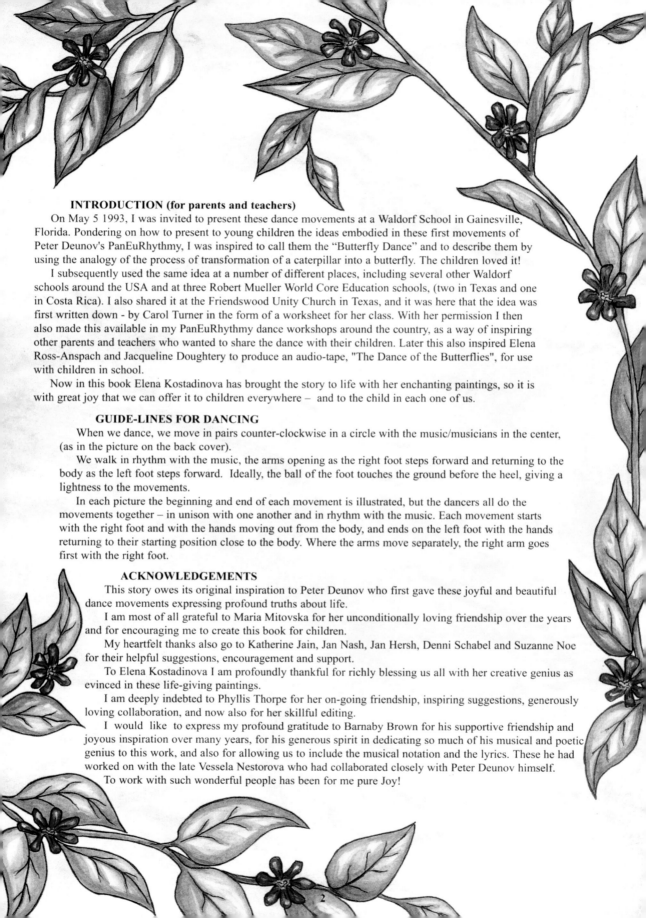

INTRODUCTION (for parents and teachers)

On May 5 1993, I was invited to present these dance movements at a Waldorf School in Gainesville, Florida. Pondering on how to present to young children the ideas embodied in these first movements of Peter Deunov's PanEuRhythmy, I was inspired to call them the "Butterfly Dance" and to describe them by using the analogy of the process of transformation of a caterpillar into a butterfly. The children loved it!

I subsequently used the same idea at a number of different places, including several other Waldorf schools around the USA and at three Robert Mueller World Core Education schools, (two in Texas and one in Costa Rica). I also shared it at the Friendswood Unity Church in Texas, and it was here that the idea was first written down - by Carol Turner in the form of a worksheet for her class. With her permission I then also made this available in my PanEuRhythmy dance workshops around the country, as a way of inspiring other parents and teachers who wanted to share the dance with their children. Later this also inspired Elena Ross-Anspach and Jacqueline Doughtery to produce an audio-tape, "The Dance of the Butterflies", for use with children in school.

Now in this book Elena Kostadinova has brought the story to life with her enchanting paintings, so it is with great joy that we can offer it to children everywhere – and to the child in each one of us.

GUIDE-LINES FOR DANCING

When we dance, we move in pairs counter-clockwise in a circle with the music/musicians in the center, (as in the picture on the back cover).

We walk in rhythm with the music, the arms opening as the right foot steps forward and returning to the body as the left foot steps forward. Ideally, the ball of the foot touches the ground before the heel, giving a lightness to the movements.

In each picture the beginning and end of each movement is illustrated, but the dancers all do the movements together – in unison with one another and in rhythm with the music. Each movement starts with the right foot and with the hands moving out from the body, and ends on the left foot with the hands returning to their starting position close to the body. Where the arms move separately, the right arm goes first with the right foot.

ACKNOWLEDGEMENTS

This story owes its original inspiration to Peter Deunov who first gave these joyful and beautiful dance movements expressing profound truths about life.

I am most of all grateful to Maria Mitovska for her unconditionally loving friendship over the years and for encouraging me to create this book for children.

My heartfelt thanks also go to Katherine Jain, Jan Nash, Jan Hersh, Denni Schabel and Suzanne Noe for their helpful suggestions, encouragement and support.

To Elena Kostadinova I am profoundly thankful for richly blessing us all with her creative genius as evinced in these life-giving paintings.

I am deeply indebted to Phyllis Thorpe for her on-going friendship, inspiring suggestions, generously loving collaboration, and now also for her skillful editing.

I would like to express my profound gratitude to Barnaby Brown for his supportive friendship and joyous inspiration over many years, for his generous spirit in dedicating so much of his musical and poetic genius to this work, and also for allowing us to include the musical notation and the lyrics. These he had worked on with the late Vessela Nestorova who had collaborated closely with Peter Deunov himself.

To work with such wonderful people has been for me pure Joy!

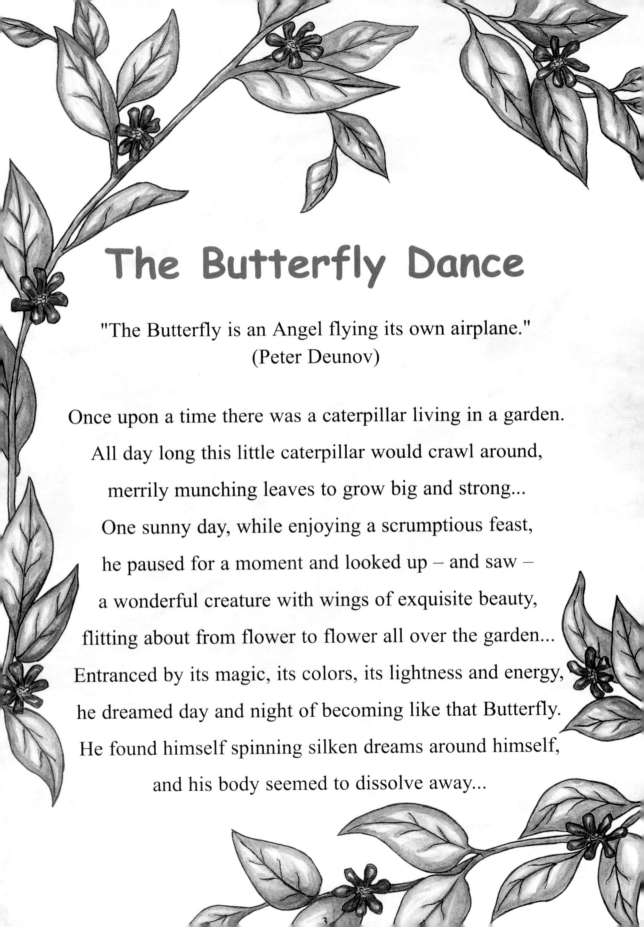

The Butterfly Dance

"The Butterfly is an Angel flying its own airplane."
(Peter Deunov)

Once upon a time there was a caterpillar living in a garden.

All day long this little caterpillar would crawl around,

merrily munching leaves to grow big and strong...

One sunny day, while enjoying a scrumptious feast,

he paused for a moment and looked up – and saw –

a wonderful creature with wings of exquisite beauty,

flitting about from flower to flower all over the garden...

Entranced by its magic, its colors, its lightness and energy,

he dreamed day and night of becoming like that Butterfly.

He found himself spinning silken dreams around himself,

and his body seemed to dissolve away...

Awakening

How could he,

with many legs, a heavy body and no wings,

ever become like that Butterfly?

At first it seemed hopeless...

Yet he remembered the Butterfly

gracefully lifting its wings,

spreading them out with such delicacy and grace.

1. Awakening,
Moderato (♩ = 60)

Voice*

1. Rise!   A - wak - en!   Spring   is   here.

O - pen your door   to   day - light   clear.

Full - ness of   life   for   ev - ery - thing

brings   the ___ first   bright   day   of   spring.

brings   the ___ first   bright   day   of   spring.

* Any part of the melody may be sung an octave higher or lower so that it lies more comfortably in the voice.
An edition for violinists and other instrumentalists is published separately.

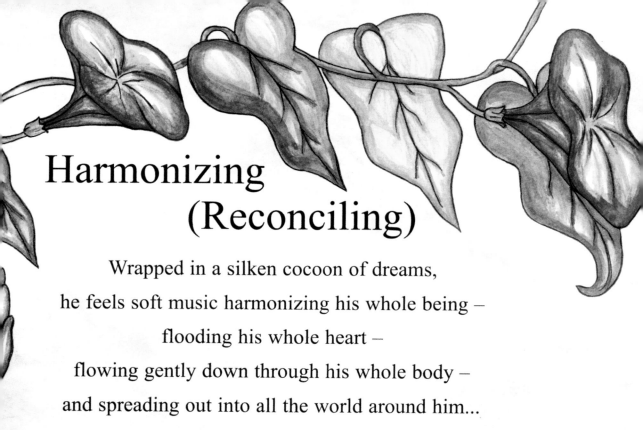

Harmonizing
(Reconciling)

Wrapped in a silken cocoon of dreams,

he feels soft music harmonizing his whole being –

flooding his whole heart –

flowing gently down through his whole body –

and spreading out into all the world around him...

2. Reconciliation,

Na - ture is smi - ling, sun is — shi - ning, hea - vens are blue.

wa - ken - ing earth to life a - new.

Flo - wers, trees and birds and bees, in

co - lours — bright and voi - ces — clear,

ce - le - brate the spring that's here.

ce - le - brate the spring that's here.

Fine

Giving

The caterpillar feels so joyful, and longs to share his joy!

He remembers the Butterfly alighting gently on the flowers:

"Ah, they were giving gifts to one another!"

Now he too wants to be giving his joy to others.

3. Giving

. Now be o - pen to re - ceive

all the bless - ings spring days _ leave,

beau - ti - ful gifts of life, thoughts bright and pure, _____

feel - ings sure, feel-ings of love that will en - dure, _____

thoughts _ as rays of sun - shine in the spring. _____

Gifts _ of gold this glad time now to us will bring. _____

Climbing (Ascending)

With his whole being the caterpillar yearns for fuller Life.

Then slowly, as if climbing a mountain,

he feels himself rising and singing with gratitude,

while inspiring new possibilities come into his life...

4. Ascending

Then look up at yon - der __ sun and hail his _ work of ___

won - der done. Sing your praise un - to the skies, a

joy - ful spar - kle in your eyes. Feel the sac - red

thrill! ___ With the birds the air with mu - sic fill. _____

Soaring (Elevation)

Now he feels himself no longer simply climbing,

but soaring up and up – on wings – just like that Butterfly!

Never before has he felt so joyful and alive!

He longs to start sharing this joy with all around him.

5. Elevation

111 both up / both down
High - er, ev - er high - er   ev - ery-one as - pire.

115
Ne - ver think to   stop   un - til   you __ reach   the

119 hands on hips
most   ex - alt - ed   moun - tain   top. _____

Opening

His heart is radiating joy and opening to LOVE.

His mind is discovering new ideas and opening to WISDOM.

On these two wings of Wisdom and Love

he starts winging his way towards TRUTH.

6. Opening

Cast off the clothes of the cold win-ter-time,

bathe in the rays of to-day's sun - shine.

Deep - ly _ breathe, ab - sorb - ing _ all in _ sight,

thank - ing _ God for the free - dom and joy of _ light. _

Shin - ing a - bove, the sun shows _ us the _ way,

fill - ing our hearts with _ joy this _ spring - time _ day,

shin - ing a - bove, the sun shows _ us the _ way,

fill - ing our hearts with _ joy this spring - time _ day. _

D.C.
for
verses
9. & 10.

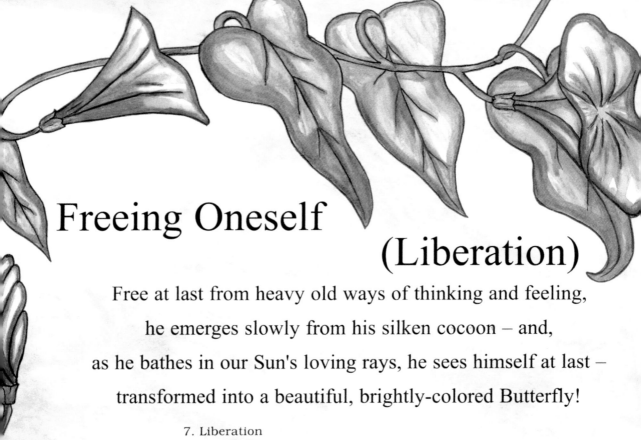

Freeing Oneself
(Liberation)

Free at last from heavy old ways of thinking and feeling,

he emerges slowly from his silken cocoon – and,

as he bathes in our Sun's loving rays, he sees himself at last –

transformed into a beautiful, brightly-colored Butterfly!

7. Liberation

Fi - nal - ly, freed   from the chains   of the past,

break - ing a - way,   li - ber - at - ed at last,

fly   o - ver lakes   to   moun - tain __ peaks   sno-wy white;

there,   at the door - step of God, fold your wings and a - light. ___

Blessed   is the soul   that,   one   with __ God,   at - tains

life   ev - er - last - ing, __ life   on __ high - er __ planes.

blessed   is the soul   that,   one   with __ God,   at - tains

life   ev - er - last - ing, __ life   on __ high - er __ planes. _

D.C.
for
verses
9 & 10

Clapping for Joy

Our new Butterfly spreads his wings in wonder and joy!

Gratitude for life springs up in his heart and

Grace flows down – through him, and out into the world...

At last his dream is coming true!!!

8. Clapping

Joy like a spring from the heart let ___ flow!

In ev - ery - thing is new life a - glow.

Share the joy, the soar - ing ___ of the _ soul;

bless ev - ery - one on your way; give your love to _ all. ___

Sing - ing the song of free - dom, _ clap your hands,

send - ing _ rays of _ joy to _ far - thest _ lands,

sing - ing the song of free - dom, _ clap your hands,

send _ ing _ rays of _ joy to _ far - thest _ lands. ___

D.C.
for
verses
9 & 10

Purifying

Blowing gentle kisses, he flits happily about the garden,

dropping soft pollen on the delighted flowers,

who gladly share with him sweet juice they create

with the help of our Sun's shining rays.

9. Purification

On the __ breath of God we rise

through - all __ clouds and stor - my skies,

pu - ri - fied y, come what may,

sow - ing __ beau - ty is our way.

sow - ing __ beau - ty is our way.

Flying

Now our Butterfly is truly flying – on flowing wings...

He feels the magic and joy of being fully alive!

And, by spreading pollen to make seeds for new plants,

he is also working with our Sun to create new Life!!

10. Flying

Fly - ing, soar - ing, sun - shine_ pour - ing in and_ through

ev - ery_ cell, we're born a - new.

Flo - wers, trees and birds and bees, in

co - lours_ bright and voi - ces_ clear,

ce - le - brate the spring that's here,

ce - le - brate the spring that's here. Fine

Blessing

The Butterfly pauses in silence to feel all these blessings...

Raising his wings, he breathes in the energy of Creation.

Then, bringing it down into his body, he murmurs:

"May Love, Peace and Joy live in our hearts for ever!"

Peter Deunov at the Rilla Lakes
where we dance in summer

36011454R00017

Made in the USA
Lexington, KY
10 April 2019